### *Surprise!*

Well! Surprise!

I wrote a gay porno book, partly as a joke, and partly because my bisexual erotica things caused some comment among friends to say I should.

I didn't think it would go anywhere, because I'm parsecs from an expert on the subject, though I do have some experience. After all, I was a professional rock guitarist with some big names in the late sixties and early seventies.

It's a week since I published *I Learned Young* – and it's doing a lot better than most of my other work.

So I'll write another.

# Contents


Author's note pg. 1

First Time Away From Home pg. 5

Meeting People pg. 13

Learning Things About Yourself pg. 27

Invitations pg. 38

Interim pg. 53

Retribution pg. 61

# About the author

CD began writing fiction in 1984 and has more than 300 books published as of 3/15/16 in SciFi, murder, orchid culture and various other fields.

He now resides Gualaca, Chiriqui, Panamá, where he continues research into epiphytic plants and plays music with friends. He loves the culture of the indigenous people and counts a majority of his closer friends among that group. He funds those he can afford through the universities where they have all excelled. "The Indios are very intelligent people, they are simply too poor (in material things and money.) to pursue higher education."

CD loves Panamá and the people, despite horrendous experiences (Free e-book; *Fading Paradise*). He plans to spend the rest of his life in the paradise that is Panamá

CD is involved in research of natural cancer cure at this time. It has proven effective in all cases, so far. It is based on a plant that has been in use for thousands of years, is safe, available, and cheap. He was cured of a serious lymphoma with use of the plant, *Ambrosia peruviana*.

Information about this cure is free on the FaceBook page Ambrosia peruviana for cancer. CD asks only that all who try it please report on its effectiveness on that group.

Author's note:

I recently published a gay porno book. I stated that it was mostly a combination of a few personal experiences and things I've witnessed, plus stories told, often in excruciating detail, by my gay friends.

I was in rock music in the late sixties and early seventies, in San Francisco, California, mostly. I was a guitarist songwriter and arranger, and worked with some of the big biggies of the time. As stated, often, we took "If you're not with the one you love, love the one you're with" a bit [that's understatement!] too far.

When I was fourteen, I had my first gay experiences. I had one experience with an older woman [at least seventeen years old!] that turned me onto the fact I *liked* sex! I *really* liked sex!

I was living in the country, by a lake, where we had a more realistic perception of such things than in the cities [closest city was Tampa, Florida]. My father was very devoutly religious. My mother was religious, but not to the extreme he was.

That had a great influence on my life and ideas. My experiences with my male friends was probably not too different than most. We would get together and talk about sex, me being one of the two who had any experience at all, get horny, jerk each other off, and end up ass fucking.

That was normal for the time and place. We never got into the oral part until I was almost fifteen, when we had an older man who taught all of us what it was liked to get a blow job. We would go to a place by the lake, and he would blow all of us, usually six or more in a day.

I am naturally a bit bi. I wondered what it would be like to suck a dick. He seemed to be in ecstacy when he sucked us. I was laying back on the hood of his car, he got me off, and would say, "More! More!'

I, of course, at that age, didn't want more for awhile. He knew that [he told us he was once our tender age, and knew how coming made you "satisfied" to where you would find it unpleasant to continue.] He would have another on the other side of the hood and would bury his face in his crotch almost immediately. He really got off when someone was ass fucking him while he sucked a couple of us off.

We all knew it was illegal, and that we would all be in neck deep shit if our parents ever found out.

He was "caught" with, luckily, a boy who was seventeen, going on eighteen. He could get a jail sentence or go to a psychiatrist. He went to a psychiatrist, who came with him to the lake a few times. He said, "See? There's nothing wrong with you!" He gave a better blow job than XXX. Slower, 'til you wanted to scream when you came.

Homosexuality was against the law, then, and with minors still is.

I agree with the "minor" part, but would have to re-define who was included. I think paedophilia should be defined as with prepubescent children, and minors defined as sexually immature. We were, all of us, the real instigators.

Where I'm living now, the Indios on the comarca are age of consent at twelve. They recognize six sexes, male homo, male hetero, female homo, female hetero, male bisexual, female bisexual.

Most are differing degrees of bisexual.

I don't know if I agree with the fact that, at around age eight, there are definite signs of which you are. I was talking with the parents of a nine year old boy who was, undeniably, coming on to me [I have very white/ blonde hair, which, next to blue eyes, turns the Indios on, big time!] They said they knew he was gay at about six years of age. At the same age, they knew his brother and sister were strictly hetero. The father said he thought Obilio liked to get ass fucked. It was alright, if I wanted to, but they would insist we use a condom. There was too much SIDA [AIDS] in Bocas.

It didn't appeal to me. Not with anyone that age, and not with a boy.

Another, about sixteen, came on to me. He was expert on getting me horny. It was at his initiative, so.... Anyhow!

I have a bit of experience, and find it pleasant, but I'm not looking for gay relationships much, but am more open as I get to be the old geezer I am now. I remember, one morning, getting out of the shower and looking in the mirror, and thinking, *Who the fuck is that old...!!*

Well, I'm a writer, not without some knowledge of the subject, so, seeing I can use the geetus, why not?

I think I like writing porn. Not so much the gay stuff, but my normal erotica with females just doesn't quite cut it. All of those had a moral.

Gay porn has an immoral, or unmoral, if you think like too many do.

Tim Andy Andrews sighed deeply and got on the bus. He was going to Evanston, the only city for more than a hundred fifty miles from Elmsburg.

Elmsburg was a small farm town in the middle of nowhere. Four hundred fourteen people, now four hundred thirteen. In an area of 640 square miles.

The recent failure of the country to consider its food supply before destroying the markets meant he had to find a job elsewhere. He was lucky that his parents had enough in the bank to hold on, and that they weren't in debt for hundreds of thousands, like most in the area. They owned the farm, and weren't about to mortgage it, which would mean losing it in a few years. They could grow what they needed to hold on.

Tim's sister had gone to Macon, Georgia, just two years ago. She had a good job with a big clothes market in the mall.

Tim was eighteen last Sunday, and said he was not going to mooch off his folks like the Adams useless bums. He was responsible for his own life, and for helping those who had raised him.

Randy Gainsborough was owner/manager of a health gymnasium in Evanston. The Happy Days Workout Center. He said Tim looked like the posters advertising the place. Those posters with the idealized bodybuilder-cum-Adonis studs.

Randy was handsome, too. He said he had to work his

ass off to be that way, but Tim just was. Randy always noticed when a guy was handsome or sexy. He noticed the women, too.

Well, he did have a good build. He did heavy labor for his whole life. As to the face, weren't those made-up features just a combination of what people looked like?

Okay. He was handsome, and knew it. It was because he never had acne or any of that, and no scars, and the sun didn't mess up his skin, like so many. The girls always came on to him, so that was a sign, too.

He had heard of queers – guys who wanted to have sex with other guys. He didn't see how anyone would want to, but his Pops had said there were all kinds of people in the world. Just because they didn't think the same way you did didn't make them wrong. They may be right, and you wrong! Maybe both could be right. After all, they weren't the same person. They didn't have the same genes and they didn't have the same influences and they didn't live the same life. If it's not what is good for you doesn't mean it's not good for them.

He said he didn't think he'd like whatever they did, but he didn't know what they liked, or why, either.

Mom was a little more religious. She said those people were terribly misguided, and that they were damned if they couldn't be made to see the light.

Uncle George, the one time it was brought up when he was there, said a person was what that person was. No man could ever be happy if he tried to live a lie. He knew two people who were queer – what they called gay – and had sex with them a couple of times, but he didn't care for it, personally, which didn't take anything away from the ones who did like it. "Try it. If you don't like it, you'll know, and don't have to do it again."

Moms was outraged, but grinned, and said she would never understand. If you never try it, you won't miss it.

He was thirteen when they said that.

He tried it with girls, and liked it! He was a bit curious about guys. He didn't really know what they did. He jerked off sometimes. There was some kind of thing that made him feel he needed to. He asked his Pops about it, and he said it's a matter of "Use it or lose it," like so many other things in life. You do it, but deny to others that you do.

Another time [he could discuss anything with Pops. Jim Horn said his pops would smack him across the room if he ever mentioned anything like sex] he asked Pops what queers did."Suck dicks. Ass fuck. Other things."

"Did you ever suck a dick?"

"No. I've had mine sucked. It felt good, but its not enough, for some reason. I liked it, but I don't want it again. Maybe if I didn't have a good sex life, I would. Don't care to find out."

"Did you ever ass fuck?"

"Yeah. When I was about fifteen or sixteen. It was ok, but not special. Sort of nasty, and you know I don't like nasty."

"You ever get ass fucked?"

"Yeah. Once. I did *not* like it. At *all*! He was bigger than me and held me down and fucked me. It hurt, and I never went anywhere near him again.

"I could have gotten him in a lot of trouble. He was nineteen and I was sixteen.

"I would never do that. I sort of knew he'd done that to another guy, but that guy let him. I'm sort of mixed. Maybe I should've. Maybe he raped others who weren't strong enough to just say, 'That kind of thing happens. It's no fault of mine.' Maybe someone else would be hurt by it. Somebody who was raised with different ideas.

"It didn't matter much. He went to prison for ten years a couple of months later. We all said now he would learn what it was like to get raped. There were a lot of men in prison a lot bigger than him.

"Listen, Tim. If anyone forces you to do anything, or fucks you when you didn't start it, you tell me."

"When I didn't start it?"

"You'll horse around with friends when you're a little older. You'll claim you never, but you will. It's part of growing up.

"You might get too hot, and do things.

"It's alright. It's a part of growing up.

"If you and a bud are horsing around and fuck each other, it's not wrong. Even if you like it, and do it a lot, it's not wrong. It happens."

"Did you do that?"

"Some. We never actually got off. We would get really hot and jerk off.

"Tim, don't ever tell the name of anyone you screw around with. It's okay to say you did this or that, but it's never okay to say you did it with Joe Doe. Same with the girls. It's okay to say you did this or that, but never okay to say, 'With Sally Jones.' Understand?"

"Yeah. You always said sex is private."

Pops was really cool! [They used that expression back then.]

*Here goes the bus. I wonder what it will be like in Evanston. I've never been away from home before!*

He got to the seat. He had a seat beside a really pretty girl – woman, she was about twenty five – who looked him over. They talked a lot, and she said she was meeting her boyfriend at Evanston. Damn it! If she ever saw a man she wanted to lay, right there in the flower bed, it was him!

He took it as a joke, but it really wasn't, and they both knew it. It was a nonstop bus, or they also both knew they would go for a fast roll at the first opportunity.

Three hours of being horny. Then, her boyfriend would meet the bus.

Bummer! What a way to be away from home the first time! Horny as hell, and nothing but his hand to do anything about it!

A fat, sort of prissy man, kept looking at him from across the aisle. He would be a queer, the way he couldn't keep his eyes off of Tim's crotch whenever the opportunity arose.

Karen noticed, and said that old queen wanted to get fucked as much as she did. By him.

"Would you?"

"No. Not because he's queer, but because I can't stand fat. That's a first turn-off for me. He's also a smoker, cigarettes in his shirt pocket. That's another turn-off.

"I don't think I would if he wasn't fat. I've never done that kind of thing before. There wasn't any of it where I was raised that I knew about."

"Hah! You could make a fortune in Evanston fucking queens. They'd pay someone like you big-time!"

He laughed. "Maybe I'll be a whore if my job doesn't work out!"

"You have a job before you ever go there?"

"Yeah. I'm going to be night manager at a gym."

"Which one?"

"Happy Days."

She raised an eyebrow. "Oh?"

"What's wrong?"

"You don't know?"

"Know what?"

"Let's just say, if you're going to be a male whore – hustler – that's the place to be to *really* make a bundle! It's known as a gay hangout."

"Oh, shit! Really?"

She laughed. "You didn't know?"

"I've never been to Evanston. A friend owns it."

"Randy?"

"Yes."

"He's not gay, I don't think. He might be bi. I know he's a great bed partner. He's a nice guy, but no promises or strings.

"How do you know him?"

"His father and mine have been friends for years. We knew each other all my life."

"He never told you about the gym?"

"Well, he said he owns it, and that there are a lot of guys there who would give their right arm to look like me. He said there are some queer customers, but he doesn't interfere in their private lives, and they don't interfere in his. Everybody to their own thing."

"I guess, if he did anything with your father, you wouldn't know.

"Is your father as handsome as you?"

He thought about it. "I guess. I never thought about it. I guess he is.

"He would have told me."

"Warn you not to be alone with Randy?"

"No. We were alone together a lot."

"He didn't try anything?"

Tim thought again. "Well, not directly. He was like all the other buds. He would tease some, and we grabbed at each other. Just playing, like. He never did anything. He said he'd like to fuck me sometimes. I said the same kind of thing. It was just guys teasing.

"I can't believe I'm saying all this to a girl I don't even know! Pops always said to *never* use a name when I talk about sex!

"I guess that's alright. I'm just telling you he never did anything but tease, like everyone else. It's not talking about sex, because there never was any."

They chatted about other things for awhile. It was a pleasant enough trip.

"We're here! Damn it! We didn't talk about anything but sex the whole way! I hope George is a tenth as horny as I am! I'll probably kill him!"

They laughed. She waved and went to hug a tall, rather handsome dark man. For the first time he was conscious of it, he looked at a man's crotch. George has a hell of a bulge. He didn't think he could do anything for Karen if what he was told was true, that a huge cock would spoil a girl for anyone with a normal one.

Well, he was a little more than normal, if all his friends were normal. Jake had the biggest. He and Fred were second. That guy had a bigger cock than Jake, unless he had, as they joked, a pair or two of socks stuffed into his jock strap!

He got off the bus and asked where Helen's Boarding House was. It was just eight blocks away. He could use a taxi. He was carrying an obviously heavy, large suitcase.

Taxi? For eight blocks? What? He was a wimp?

He grinned and headed for the boarding house.

Surprise! "Helen" was a sour, grouchy, fat old man with an attitude.

Tim found the gym was just six blocks away, so called Randy and said he'd be over in a little while. Randy said they had the special group tonight, so it would be better if he waited until the next day. He would cause a riot if it was announced that the new manager, who never went to a gym in his life, was in better condition that those who had been going for years.

"Met Helen?"

"Yeah. That was a surprise. I never pictured Helen as an old, fat, greasy slob with a sour attitude!"

They both laughed. "You should see him when he's not in one of his better moods!"

"I don't think I'll take any meals here if he cooks. I'd go apeshit if I went into the kitchen, right? Piles of old food in the corner. Dirty dishes all over the place. Rancid grease in every pan..."

"It would be another surprise! The kitchen makes a hospital look like a pig stye. Not a speck of grease any-where. Garbage is _outside_, in the sealed bins. The rooms are as clean. If you want to see a _really_ bad mood, leave a mess somewhere."

"Really?"

"Really. He's a gourmet chef. If you eat there much, you'll get fat."

"Is there anyplace you'd suggest to go to meet people here?"

"I ... don't know what to suggest. Things here aren't the

same as Podunkville. I have to explain about a lot of what you'll see and hear. I couldn't tell you about it back home. It's ... different. I might have made a mistake bringing you here."

"I sat with Karen on the bus here. She told me some things."

"Tim, you do *not* do anything you don't agree with. *That* is written in stone. The meeting here tonight is what you would almost call a gay orgy. You do *not* have to go to any such thing. Your job is to manage a gym. Period. No 'extra duties' or any of that shit. That will be up to you. Absolutely."

"I never thought it would be, even when Karen told me the gym is a hangout."

"She talked that much with you? A stranger?"

He laughed. "She started with saying she wanted me to fuck her right there in the flower patch!"

"Did she think you were to be a club whore?"

"No. She said I could make a ton of money if I did."

He could hear the laughter in Randy's voice.

"How did you answer that?"

"It might work out fine! I would have to see if I could even ... perform with the gay crowd."

"You surprise the shit out of me! I should expect it, knowing your father. He's as blunt, and as practical.

"See you here at nine in the morning?"

"Nine? The middle of the day?"

Randy laughed. "This is the big – well medium-size – city! We wake up at eight, not four. After what tonight will probably be, I'll still be dead tired, but life has to go on!"

"Do you perform at the que ... gay scene?"

"I perform at any scene, almost. I'm a bisexual sex addict.

"You can say 'queer'. It's not really a put-down, in that sense."

They chatted a minute, then Tim went down to dinner. It really was as good as Randy said it would be. There were three other boarders there. There were eight, in all, but only the four of them that night. The three seemed to be regular older guys. They were three retired men with pensions.

Helen [that was really his name! "My mother wanted a girl."] warmed up a bit when he hinted at what kind of job Tim had at "That place." Tim said, "Manager. No extra duties. Personal activities are personal, and have no bearing on it."

Kyle, the oldest of the bunch, said, "You're so fucking good looking you'll triple their business by just being there. Owner's not stupid, but he's sex crazy. He'll come on to you. What then?"

"I've known him all my life. He's never said anything to me, except joking, when he said he wanted to fuck me. We both knew it was a joke that was true, but it would never happen."

"Never's a long time. You get older and do things you always swore you wouldn't."

"Could we maybe talk about something else?" Helen requested. "You know how I am about that gay shit."

So they talked about a lot of things. It was a pleasant

enough dinner.

Kyle, Leon, and Gene were nice enough people. Even Helen wasn't nearly as bad as Tim had thought he would be.

After the meal, Tim said he was going to walk around and get to know Evanston. Were there any particular places to avoid?

Gene said, "So you can check them out to see if they're really all that bad?"

They all laughed. "Probably."

Happy Harry's. Pink Rabbit. He'd probably meet everyone there at the gym. Pink was a lesbian joint.

"I didn't mean gay joints. Rough places. Bikers and that."

"You're big enough and fit enough they won't give you any shit," Leon said. "Harley Haven is the bikers' place, but they're not half as tough as they want you to think. I wouldn't be surprised if you met a lot who go to the gym there."

"Our queens here aren't the scared pussy type. They can pretty well kick shit out of the wannabe thugs here."

Tim waved and headed to the park, thought that would be a bad idea. He'd heard enough about parks.

He went into the Log Cabin for a beer, where he met Desiree, who said she was a pro, but maybe a free sample for a special person?

He declined. He met Leona, who wasn't as bimbo-like, but was pretty.

They spent a couple of great hours at her place, then he went to the boarding house.

In the morning, he headed for the gym.

"Well! You look fit and ready!" Randy, who had an obvious serious hangover, greeted.

"Had a great night! Got laid on my first night here!"

"I'd say we should look around, but you really look like warmed-over hell!"

"Drank too much, and poppers. Play the song and pay the piper!"

"Why don't you use guava leaf extract so you don't get a hangover? I don't know what poppers are. Maybe it wouldn't work with them."

"Amyl nitrite. Make a good orgasm fantastic! To some. Some of us don't like them.

"What's that guava stuff? I had guava syrup on my pancakes. Didn't do anything for a hangover."

"It's something a guy in Panama put on a forum. Make a tea. It works! You have to use the leaves.

"So! What now? I'm here!"

"You come on at four and work 'til we close at eleven. You can look over the programs we use. If you know a better one, we'll try it.

"They come in, you have them sign in if they're members, or collect for the use by the hour. Gina and Will run the programs. You arrange for times.

"The general users usually sign up and pay by the month or quarter. They come in and use the equipment on the main floor.

"Oh! You assign lockers to anyone who doesn't have one. Only the longer term clients have one that they leave stuff in.

"You will get some complaints from people who get approached in the showers or rest rooms. Even the locker room. Tell them that all they have to do is say,"No,' and that handles it, unless they put their hands on you, in which case you smack them in the puss.

"None of the regulars will cause a problem. We have a code about that, and they know they can be booted if they break it.

"Same applies to you. Say, "no,' then kick their ass if they go too far.

"Tim, a lot will want to touch you. You're a doll!

"It's up to you how you handle it. You already know we have a lot of gay clients.

"Another thing about that. A lot of teenagers come here. Most of them want a gay romp, but *not* here. Period!

"Now, this is the dance room where Gina...."

Tim knew every nook and cranny in the place, and knew the uses Randy would tolerate. There were cameras in most of them. The clients weren't to know that, unless someone tried to rape someone else or something, in which case he was to "accidently" show up.

"You're going to see things you definitely are *not* going to believe, particularly with people you would *not* expect to be doing those things.

"I know I can trust you. If anyone tries to get any of the videos – and very few know about them – to blackmail someone, I'll have them hit.

"I mean it. The type knows how I am, so I've never had a problem.

"Do not sign anything that says a specific person was here at a specific time, except the regulars, and they won't be the type anyone would blackmail. Tell anyone who asks that the register book can be looked at by any authorized agency, and they ain't no authorized agency.

"Pretty clear?"

Tim grinned. "Like last night? And it's *you* I want to blackmail?"

"Well ... I don't remember ... how about we check out last night? I don't think there's anything that could be used in blackmail. It would be if it was with someone who could be blackmailed about something on that order that happened with thirty two others watching!

"Here's the recording section."

Randy and Tim stepped inside the office, and Randy locked the door. No one was there when they went into the office.

They went into a room behind the office through a doorway that was hidden behind the row of file cabinets. Randy opened the drawer marked "I-J-K" and pulled a tab on the lever between J and K. He then pulled the cabinets forward to reveal the door. There were four active computer screens, each showing four pictures per screen. There was another blank screen.

"That's to the private cubicles and such. The main ones are under the counter out front, and the clients know about them. They can see them from the end. They probably don't know that we can change each shot from four angles. Maybe they do. The four cameras are right there."

He pulled out two memory sticks from the computer that was turned off. "They're on timed circuits. They start when the place officially closes and run until the lights are turned off anytime after three thirty. We've never run past that."

He put labels on the sticks, and put one back in the USB port and turned the comp on. After a minute to warm up, he clicked on the icon, and the screen lit up with six pictures of people coming in the door and going to a side door. Randy said that was to the locker room. There were four cameras there, too, but everyone knew about them. They didn't know about the six in the room.

The men came back out of the locker room, nude, and went to the little bar set up to one side. They mixed drinks, opened sodas, poured juice [the most used] or took a beer from the cooler, then started circulating. Some of them kissed when they met. Tim had never seen a man kiss another man like that. He grinned and adjusted his shorts.

Now some of them were feeling others up. One of them, a guy about twenty, was sucking on another, a guy maybe thirty's, nipples.

It was in screen number two, and the shots weren't very good that small. Randy asked if he wanted to see any particular screen, so he said that one. He'd never seen it before, and the guy seemed to be getting a really *big* hard-on!

Randy clicked on the screen. It was now the only one, and was the whole screen. The younger guy slowly kissed the older one's chest and was running his tongue all over his stomach. The guy was groaning and had a hand on the head of the younger one. He was pushing him down. He was getting his balls sucked, then his dick. They went to a massage table, The older one sat, and the younger one was sucking him. He was moaning, after a minute, and the one sucking him was getting faster, and was swallowing the whole dick.

Tim didn't see how anyone could ... Randy said it was a deep throat. not everyone could take that much cock all the way.

The sound was general, and not much could be heard clearly from the individual spot, but the expression on the guy's face didn't need sound.

"That's Ken, doing the sucking. Arny is getting off on it big time! He must have to leave early, or he'd stop before ... Ghee! Is he getting off or *what*!"

Ken pushed his face hard into Arny's crotch, and held for about ten seconds – ten seconds of pure ecstacy on Arny's face.

Randy zoomed in on Arny. He slowly raised from the crotch, stopped to very lightly suck about halfway out, and finished with a "lollipop" as Randy called it, where he sucked for a minute on just the head. Ken jerked, and looked like he was going to faint.

They both straightened up. They kissed, and Arny went to another very muscular man ["That's Kitt. He's fun!"], who laughed and grabbed him to force him to go down on him. Arny sucked for a minute, then straightened up and bent over the massage table. Kitt slid on a condom, then ass fucked Arny, who had his eyes closed and a look of ecstacy on his face.

Randy clicked again and the six scenes were there. All six screens had men is many positions. Two were now ass fucking others, one of whom was sucking another. Three guys were laying in a sort of circle, each sucking another one. One was sucking two, who was sucking three, who was sucking one.

Tim had a hard-on like he seldom had before. "I'm actually turned on! Cripes!"

Three big men were forcing a fourth against a frame. They were tying his hands and feet to the frame, making a spread eagle. He was trying to fight them, but they were too much for one person to fight.

One of the ones tying him sucked on his chest for a few seconds, then went to twist his head around and kiss him. He was still struggling, but slower and slower. The guy kissing him was feeling his [very stiff] prick, massaging, then squeezing his balls a little.

"I thought you didn't allow rape?" Tim asked.

"It's his thing. He likes the dominance bit. He's been here before, and they actually probably raped him, but he didn't object. He really got into it. Probably not as much as he did last night.

"Tim, he came here on his own. He's gay, and was trying to deny it. He wouldn't have come if he wasn't. He would have come to me, at least, or to the police, if it was actual rape.

"He wouldn't go to the police, if it was. He would have to admit that it was probably the best night of his life.

"Watch. You'll see how he gets into it. He wants

nothing more in life than to do the things he'll do. Maybe he'll want the dominance bit again, but maybe he'll see this is what he needs."

The one who kissed him went down and was sucking him. Another went behind and put on a condom. ["We insist on a condom. Always, with an ass fuck."] The guy was twisting, but not too much. It was plain he expected to get fucked, and wanted it.

After about four or five minutes [during which Tim saw a lot of other things going on, like a throat fuck on a massage table. *That* one was pulling the "top" down hard, and was really enjoying it.] Tim shook his head and grinned.

"Too much for you?" Randy asked.

"No. I was thinking maybe I'd like to fuck that guy in the mouth if he likes it that much. I know I would!"

Back to the frame. Another of the ones who tied him had climbed the frame to push his dick into the guy's face. He tried to turn away, and the fourth forced his mouth open with his thumbs. The prick was inserted. The guy choked a little, fought for a second, then was still, then was sucking.

Tim moved his own prick to a more comfortable position, and was massaging it. Randy grinned. He was obviously as stimulated. "Want to fuck? Suck?"

Tim giggled.

The one ass fucking him threw his head back and made a noise they couldn't hear. The guy was sucking in earnest. He was faster and faster, and he obviously came. The one he was sucking stayed there for about a minute and a half more, then came. The guy coughed, and some cum ran from the corner of his mouth. The one he was sucking stayed there where he couldn't back off for a few seconds, then slowly withdrew.

The guy bent forward and didn't stop sucking. It stayed that was for about a half minute more, then the guy withdrew all the way. The one who had been sucking him moved to kiss him passionately for a minute.

"He gets a mouthful of his own cum. That's sort of traditional. He still has some of Curt's cum in his mouth. Now, he'll swallow it all. Ben will swallow his part."

Another guy came to behind and was ass fucking him.

"He'll get several more. He wants it, but they should untie him and let him go to a massage table."

Tim watched as four guys in a row were ass fucking. "It's hard to move if you're one of the ones in the middle," Randy said. "God! I'm hot – and it's not them! I want to fuck you. You can fuck me. Please!" He was rubbing Tim's cock. Tim tried to not ... then said, "Okay. I guess I'll have to see if I like it someday, and there's no time like the present!"

He opened his pants and stepped out of them. Randy slipped his arms under Tim's tee shirt and lifted it, then pulled it off. He dropped his own pants and grabbed Tim's cock. He massaged and jerked it a bit, then slid behind. He picked up a tube of body oil, said, "You'll need lubrication, the first time."

He was inserting his cock. It hurt!

No, it didn't. Not even as much as when he was con-stipated that one time. He felt it go deeper, then felt a sensation that was like just the beginning of an orgasm. He gasped.

"Direct stimulation of the prostate. Some feel it a lot, and some don't feel it at all. If it's too much, I'll stop."

Tim shook his head. This wasn't at all like he thought it would be! It felt good, in some ways. After a few minutes, Randy got faster and faster, then came. Tim was surprised at how it felt, even with the tipped condom. He didn't know you had feeling that far up your ass!

He was on the verge of coming. Randy slipped a condom on him, and said to go to it! He wished this had been happening for the past five years!

Tim came fairly fast, but he was ready before he got to do the fucking. He held to Randy tightly for a couple of minutes, barely moving, after he came.

He withdrew and kissed Randy. His first time to kiss a man on the mouth. It was kinky and fun.

"Well. Now you know if you like it." Randy said. "I know I did!

"We'd better get to the job. This isn't part of it, Tim. I want to fuck with you a lot, but it's not part of the job. We've been friends for years without it. If you don't want it, we can still be friends for a lot more years."

Tim kissed him again. "I don't know how much I'll want it, but I'll want it."

They dressed. Randy kissed him. They held tightly for a minute, then went back into the office. Gina was just outside the door, at the desk. "Oh! I didn't know you were here! I [she saw Tim] oh."

"Gina, Tim. Tim's going to be night manager."

"God! He's as much of a dream as you said! I wish he liked women!"

"Oh, I do! A lot!"

They talked awhile. Tim met Will. People were coming in, so he said he'd be back at four and went back to the boarding house. Arny, from last night's video, was staying there!

Tim went to the office, where Randy showed him where everything was. There were about twenty people working out, more than half of whom were in a diet/exercise class with Gina.

Randy would leave at five, and come back at about a quarter to eleven or so. He might stay after the place closed, depending on ... things.

Someone new would come in about every ten minutes, and the ones already there would leave. The class left at the same time. Gina came to say she would be back at seven for her class. Will came to chat. He introduced Tim to Tommy, who was an apprentice instructor.

"Did Randy tell you about the special classes after hours on most Wednesdays and Saturdays?"

"He said there were sort of semi-private orgies in the exercise room."

Tommy giggled. Tim recognized him, vaguely, as being on one of the massage tables, getting ass fucked.

"Before you come to any conclusions, I don't attend. I'm married, and am very happy with it," Will said. "Tommy, you go to them, don't you?"

"Sometimes."

"You going to be going to them?" Will seemed to have a little bit of an attitude. Tommy rolled his eyes where Tim couldn't see.

"I doubt it. I'm not the orgy type, particularly not a gay orgy."

"I don't mean to sound judgmental. Most of the particularly handsome men here go to them. Tommy does, as he just said."

"If it's your thing, go for it!" Tim replied. "It's not mine. If Tommy gets off on it, more power to him. I hope he gets all he wants from who he wants."

"You like women?" Tommy asked.

"A lot!"

"Shit!"

They all laughed. It seemed forced with Will.

"I guess I might like sex with a guy. There wasn't any such thing where I grew up. That I knew of, of course. It's everywhere there are people. Pops told me something about it. He got a few blow jobs when he was fourteen or fifteen. He said it was okay, but he didn't want anymore. He said you had to try it to know if you liked it. He tried it. He didn't like it – but he didn't *dis*like it, either."

"Your *father* said to try it?" Will was aghast.

"No. That would be up to me. He knew I had fucked two girls, so I *knew* I liked that!"

"You told your *father* about that sex stuff?!" Will cried.

"I lived on a farm. I saw 'sex stuff' all my life. Pops is practical. He knew those things would happen in life. It happens to everybody. He just didn't try to deny it. He said my buds and I would jerk each other off, probably even ass fuck each other. I'd have a more honest life if I admitted it."

"My father would go ballistic if I ever even hinted I'd even thought about, much less done any of that stuff!" Will cried. "God! I wish he had been like yours!

"It's true. Don and I jerked each other off one time. It scared me so much that Dad might find out I never did it again! I still haven't gotten over feeling guilty about it."

"There's another thing Pops always said. Never give a name. It's alright to say a guy I knew and I jerked each other off. It's never alright to say Joe Doe and I jerked each other off."

"You and your father really get along, don't you? You're pals as well as father and son."

"I love Pops more than anyone in the world, except Moms.

"You know, I remember once when I asked Pops if I had a big dick. He said to whip it out and get a hard on, and he'd see."

"I can't even imagine letting my Dad look at my cock! Cripes!"

"Do you?" Tommy asked. "I mean, you do. I can see that!"

"A friend has a bigger one. Another friend and I are next, with about the same. I'm bigger than any of the others."

"Geesh! I can't believe I'm talking about this!" Will said. "I never showed my prick to anyone! Not even my buddies! I don't even take a shower here if anyone else is here! I could never compare ... I wouldn't get a hard on! I'd shrink up to nothing!"

"You do. I saw you coming out of the shower," Tommy said. "You're no elephant dick, but you're nice, and a little more than average."

"Oh, God! I never knew you ... I'm fucked up, aren't

I?"

"No. You're you. Your father indoctrinated that into you, mine, I guess, indoctrinated some things into me."

"Well, it's nice to meet you," Will said. "You know something? I've said that to a thousand people, and you're the first I meant it!" He went out. Tommy asked, "Wanna fuck?"

Tim laughed. "Shit! I have to get to work!"


Tim noticed several who came in who were at the orgy. Every one of them looked him over completely, when others weren't looking. He noticed men's crotches for the first time, in that way. When he went to dinner, one was the waiter at the restaurant, and one was the chef.

Randy came in at a quarter to eleven, and asked how it went. He told a little about the conversation with Will. Randy laughed, and said he knew Pops very well, and that it would shock the holy living Hell out of Will that anyone could be that open and realistic.

"I knew Will's father. He was the super pious holier than thou type. I doubt he even slept in the same bed as Joanne, his wife since Will was born. It would be Satan's own evil to have sex for any reason other than having a child.

"Will's repressed. I once thought that getting him in an orgy would be the best thing that could happen to him.

"I'm damned glad it never happened. It would destroy him."

Tim nodded. "I wonder what happened to his father to make him that way."

"*His* father."

Tim nodded.

Tim stopped for a beer on the way home. Leona was there. Tim didn't get to the boarding house until three thirty. It was a great night, if a bit confusing.

Tommy had flatly asked to get fucked. Randy didn't say or do anything, but it was clear he would like a bit of a romp in the locker room.

A video of him having sex? Would he...? It would be kinky, but he didn't think so. He got excited at the videos, but didn't think he'd want to be in any of them.

Still...?

Maybe with Leona. Not with Randy or Tommy.

Was he going to end up in a video? He had at least ten offers today, two of them from women [married. *That* was a strict no-no!], and it was a slow day. Thursdays and Mondays were the slowest for the gym, according to Randy and Gina.

Would he ever do ... well, Randy had fucked him.

Did he like it?

In a way.

Could he suck a dick?

That, he didn't know. Watching the orgy made him wonder, because so many seemed to like sucking a dick more than anything else in the world.

Cum in his mouth? Would he vomit?

Arny certainly hadn't.

He was laying there with a hard on, just thinking about it, so he guessed it was possible.

He had some very strange dreams about running from

someone. He passed a mirror, and he was running from himself!

He was well-rested in the morning, though.


"You drive me crazy!" Kitt said, leaning over the counter. "You're the sexiest guy I ever saw! God, but you are *gorgeous*!

"Now, you probably didn't have any idea, but I'm gay. No! Really!"

Tim laughed. "Well, I'm booked solid for the next two weeks. Maybe between nine and ten, Friday, two weeks?"

Kitt looked confused. "If you're hustling, how much? You're on!"

Tim laughed. "I'm just joking. I don't think I want that."

"If you said five hundred bucks, I'd agree. I'm serious."

"I'm don't like whores, as Desiree figured when I turned down a freebie. I very damned certainly would never *be* one!

"Kitt, I never had any experience with the gay stuff back home. There was never any, that I knew about. I have to wait to know if I want to know more than I do."

"You grew up with *Randy*, and never ...?"

"A couple of people reacted like that. Randy's a sex addict. We were together when I was a kid until I was eighteen, and we never did anything but tease."

"Christ! I was sucking dick when I was ten! Someone like Randy, I would have lasted ten minutes, maximum!

"The offer's open, and is going to stay open."

Tim laughed. Mrs Donlevy came to sign in, and Kitt went off toward the exercise room.

Tim didn't want any rough sex. It would be that with Kitt. It wasn't going to happen. If he did anything, it was going to be the slower, more sensual things.

Two members came in together. They hadn't been on the video, but they both gave Tim the come-on. They weren't in nearly as good shape as most. Tim looked at the histories, and saw they had been members for more than four years.

"I'm Thomas Evergreen, and he's Roland Felon. We don't play silly games. We ask what we want!"

"We want you," Roland finished. "You work here, so we know you're available. How much?"

"Will's available? I'm not a whore, and I only go with who I want. You ain't it. I just turned down five hundred for a half hour.

"Will you be using the ... [he looked them over. Flabby] I guess not.

"I go with people who take care of themselves. You obviously don't, so I would ask why you're members here, if I gave a flying fuck, but it's obvious. You want guys who take care of themselves.

"Use the stuff you've paid for. It might make your wants a lot more available."

They went away with sour backward glances. Tommy, who was just to the side, said they offered him a hundred dollars, which he refused. Same reasons Tim did.

"They're the type who hang around the park. They're rich, and think they can buy anything they want. They give me the creeps. I think they go after the little kids at the park.

"I don't mean the teenagers. I mean the little kids."

"Then they should be put against a wall and shot. Teenagers know what they want. Little kids don't." He and Tommy did a palm slap.

It wasn't an eventful day. Tommy said he wanted Tim to stay with him tonight. Tim thought about it. "If I'm strictly pitcher, why not? I'll see what it's like!"

Tommy was there when Randy came in. He raised an eyebrow. "I'm giving a special class to a couple of friends. I was going to ask if you wanted to join us?"

"Not tonight. I have a date."

Randy laughed. "Slow and easy, Tommy. He's learning. It will be heaven for you. Make it as good for him. No kinky stuff."

Tommy laughed. "It's already heaven because he said he'd go with me. I know you'll understand if I come in late tomorrow!"

"Within reason."

They had a few more laughs, then Tim went with Tommy for a snack at Dinah's before going to Tommy's room.

"It true you've never done anything? I mean, the gay stuff," Tommy said.

"Well, I kissed a guy a couple of times, and I fucked him and he fucked me. That's all."

"Randy?"

"I would never give a name!"

"Hah! Randy would love for everyone to know he was

your first! You can use my name anytime you like!

"Let's shower and all that. I want it to be fresh and clean all the way."

They undressed and got in the cool shower. Tommy lathered Tim completely and washed him. It was a great feeling. He washed Tommy, but stopped before his dick. Tommy didn't stop. Tim was getting a hard on. Tommy already had one.

They dried each other, and got in bed. Tim laid back. He didn't know what was expected of him. He might, if it was at the orgy, but this was different, and was more personal.

Tommy laid tight against him, his head on Tim's chest. He turned his head up and Tim kissed him, then he started nibbling at Tim's chest and sucking very lightly on his nipples. He was massaging his balls. He was moving down his body, tongue finding some wildly sensitive spots. Tim moaned, after a few minutes, and found himself with his hand on Tommy's head, lightly, then a bit more, pushing him down.

Tommy took Tim's dick in his mouth with an, "Mmm" sound. He was sucking very lightly in a pumping way. Tim's breath was coming in short gasps. He moaned again.

Tommy did a slow deep throat, stayed down all the way, with the slight pumping motion. This was what they called a "soak," according to Randy.

Tim's thoughts were coming is swirls of colors and sensation. It was building. Tommy was slowly drawing him in and out, just a couple of inches.

God! He never knew anything like this! He was going to ... come! He'd never known a getting off half that complete! That massive!

The sensation was getting too strong. Tommy sensed it, and stopped, just a halfway soak for a minute, then he sighed deeply, and laid his head on Tim's chest, making that little sound he'd only heard twice before. From two girls, when they were completely satisfied.

Next thing either knew, the alarm bell was going off. Tommy went down for a quick, sensuous second round, then they got up and went for a rinse in the shower, then dressed.

"I'm in love with you," Tommy said. "Oh, I know it will pass, but, right now, I'm so in love with you I can't think. I've never been so completely satisfied in my life!"

"I feel a lot of affection for you. I really like just laying there with your head on my chest and sleeping.

"Isn't that weird? I know how it feels when I'm asleep!"

They kissed, then dressed and went to Dinah's for breakfast. Tommy went to the gym, Tim went to Helen's. He spent the rest of the day until time for work shopping. He was going to be here awhile, so bought some things.

He bought shaving supplies and toothpaste and such in the pharmacy. He was going to checkout when he stopped to think, then took a box of condoms from the rack. He put it all on the counter. The girl there hadn't taken her eyes off of him since he came in. She picked up the condoms, and said, "Do you buy condoms often?"

"No. First time, really. Why?"

"Because these things will strangle you, if that package is all you. You need the silver package. These would be alright if you had a four or five inch penis. I'd estimate you need the seven through nine size.

"And what are your plans for tonight?"

He laughed. "I'll be at work. Bad luck all day!"

They joked for awhile. She said she was serious about bedding him. Anytime that was convenient would do! She got off work at four.

"And I go to work at four. Like I said, some days, nothing goes right."

He exchanged the condoms. The woman who came to the counter as he handed Daniela the condoms sniffed, and looked shocked. Daniela looked at his crotch, then at the woman, and grinned. The woman let out a small barking laugh, and said, "You got me that time! I'm just jealous!"

Tim went back to Helen's to get ready for work.

Tim was getting into the routine. He had been there a week, and had slept with Tommy another time, and with Leona, and with Daniela once. He slept with Randy once, and Arny, when Arny sneaked into his room at two in the morning. Randy had fucked him. None of the others. Kitt had tried to kiss him in the locker room, but he said, very frankly, that he was turned off with the rough stuff.

"Rough? What do you mean?"

"Er, Randy and two others said you want rough sex. You tried to force me to kiss you. I need a map?"

"I'm really sorry. I do want you – and I really am into dominance.

"I'll leave you alone, but anytime ... I'll try to not make it rough. I really want you, but, is it true, you only pitch?"

"Yes."

"Well ... I'm into both. If you ever get horny and change your mind, I'll be catcher, only."

Tim reached to kiss him quickly and lightly. "I always want it soft – not that! – and sensual."

"My god! I don't believe it! I actually felt like I was going to faint! My god! I *swooned*!"

Tim laughed and went back to check the dance class. Gina raised an eyebrow, seeing him come, followed that close by Kitt. He grinned and shook his head, "No." She said, later, that she'd never seen Kitt looking so much like a whipped puppy.

Thursday, he went into the locker room and Gene was

there. Tim had been watching a sexy girl on the bicycles. She was sexy as all Hell, and he was a little horny, which showed.

Gene reached to grab him and pull him to stand right in front of him as he sat on the bench. Gene didn't say anything, but pulled his shorts down and took his dick into his mouth, to do a deep throat, then to suck in earnest. It didn't take long for him to get off.

That was a good suck. Tim felt really good, and went back to the counter to enter the figures into the computer. The sexy girl came to lean on the counter, her tee shirt stretched tight across her chest. Tim noticed the rounded tops of her tits, and knew they were false. Implants. With her makeup running down her face, she was a long way from pretty, as she seemed from a distance, and she wasn't sexy anymore.

"I just don't know what I'm going to *do* this afternoon! My boyfriend is out of town for the week, and I just don't have anything to *do*! I'm all alone and lonely, and don't know what I'm going to *do*!" She leaned across the counter and pulled the tee shirt tighter.

"Yeah. I know how it feels. I have to work half the night, then there's nobody but the guys from here to buddy with. We do find things to *do*!"

She looked disgusted. "So I've heard.

"Is my bill paid up?"

He checked. "Through the tenth."

She walked away, stopping to look thoughtful, then went on. She stopped at the door to the women's locker, and looked back at him.

He grinned and shook his head, "No."

He thought about it. Leona was great! Daniela was good, but not that special. Randy was great! Tommy was great! Arny was good, but not really special.

Kitt would be like that woman. Wanting to be in charge, and wanting to own him.

All-in-all, he liked the guys better than the women, and a guy wasn't going to get pregnant. Maybe he was ready to try some new things. As Pops said, "If you don't like it, don't do it again." Like Randy, he could have both.

He finished the day. Randy came in for a couple of minutes. There was a woman in his car. "Here's the keys. Close for me? I have another set of keys, so you don't have to open in the morning."

"Okay. Fair enough. Get a piece for me!"

"If I can get a piece *from* you I'll tell Irene to take a hike!"

They laughed, and Randy went out. Tim closed, and stopped for his regular snack at Dinah's. Two girls were sitting at another table, and kept trying to catch his eye. He pretended not to see them. When they went out, he heard one say, "He's working at Happy. They say it's a gay hangout. Why are all the guys you want to fuck gay or married? Shit!"

"He's not gay. He slept with Daniela. She said he's the dream that got away. Randy sleeps with anybody. I've slept with him. He says he likes sex with the gays. He's really great in bed!

"Maybe he's bi. Like Randy."

"Bi or gay or whatever, I want him to fuck me to

exhaustion!"

They went out.

Was that for his benefit? Did they know he was that close?

When he checked out, he saw the little mirror by the door. They knew he was there. So! They let him know they were available, whether he likes men or not! Cool!

Did anyone say that anymore?

He went to Helen's and to bed. This time, the door was locked. No more sneaky stuff there. Helen would throw him out in a blink!

Maybe not. He knew Arny was gay.

Did Arny have sleepover guests? Would Helen put up with that?

Well, all of them had surprised him, at times. He wouldn't be surprised, either way, with Helen.


Saturday. Randy [and ten others] said there was going to be a private party tonight. If he would like to come, he was the most invited one there!

"Tim, think about it, okay? I think you're strong minded enough not to be bothered if you go too far. With you, no one will object if it's all one way, but you might go with that intention, but it wouldn't hold after you get so hot you don't know what you're doing.

"I know it won't bother you to get fucked. You told me you liked it. I don't know how you'd react to more."

"It wouldn't bother me. I've kind of wondered what it would be like. I can see from what goes on in the special rooms how a guy who goes to just get a blow job gets too involved, and some other guy gets sucked by him.

"Some, it's just part of the deal. Some seem really scared by it.

"I love a blow job. There are times when, if I'm getting a good one, I would probably suck a dick, if it's on somebody I think is sexy and clean.

"I don't know what a load of cum in my mouth would be like.

"Like pops says, 'If you don't like it, don't do it again.' I can live with that philosophy."

"Well, you'll have plenty time to shower and all that. Saturdays, most of the business is gone by ten or ten thirty. I'll be here, so you can get a good dinner. High-energy!"

"Sounds like a plan. Maybe not a good one, but a plan."

"I'll turn off the cameras."

"No. If there's anything on them I don't want out, we can erase it."

"Fair enough."


Earl, Sam, and Jon were there at closing. They went with Tim to Dinah's, had a good meal, and went back to the gym. They went to the side loading platform and inside, to the lockers, and back out to the exercise room.

In the lockers, Sam looked at Tim as he stepped out of his clothes.

"You know, I sort of dreamed of seeing you naked. I thought it would be a thrill, that you looked as good with nothing on as you did in those tight clothes.

"I was wrong!"

"*Wrong*! Are you kidding?! *Look* at him! He's a *god*!"

"That's what I mean! He's not *as* good looking nude! He's a thousand percent *better* looking!

"You two go out and mingle. I don't think I want to ever leave this room while he's in it!"

They teased and joked as they went into the gym. Randy was there, and said, "Hi! Welcome to the happiest night you will ever have!

"Well, the gayest!"

Everyone looked when he said "Hi!" There was silence.

"Well! *That* has to be the best grand entrance I've ever seen!" Earl quipped. Several laughed. They descended on Tim, who asked Randy, "What do I do now?"

Randy rubbed his cock. "Just stand there. I'll charge five bucks a feel! I'll take in a million or so!"

He laughed, grabbed Randy, and kissed him passionately.

"Kiss *me* like that, and you're a thousand dollars richer in minutes!" someone cried.

"One five!" another yelled.

They started joking and laughing. Kitt grabbed him and sat him on a massage table – and buried his face in his crotch. He was licking his balls and rubbing his dick all over his face. Someone yelled. "My turn!" and two big guys pulled Kitt away. Another was licking him and sucking. Kitt tackled one of the one who pulled him away, and shoved him down by another massage table and was forcing him to suck. The other came up behind and started ass fucking him.

Then the party really got started!

It was a blur, and a very sharp memory. He was being sucked a lot. He kissed several of the guys. They were massaging and licking all over his body. Somebody sucked on his toes [he didn't like that].

Then a sharper memory. Stan was pulling him down to sit in his lap. He was on a low stool. He was being ass fucked, but not with any movement. Soaking. Kitt was sucking him, but slowly 'Like you like." his chest was being massaged. He was laying back with his eyes closed, in a whirlpool of sensation. Someone was kissing him, then stood to put his dick against his mouth.

Well, he was here to learn if he would like to suck a dick. It seemed he would soon know. He didn't resist, but took the cock in his mouth. He sucked lightly. It was being pressed deeper.

He remembered thinking, *It's a good thing it's a small dick! I couldn't take a big one.*

It was a strange feeling. he remembered how good it felt when someone played with his balls while sucking. He reached up to massage the balls right there. Someone put a big cock in his other hand.

He was building. Sensation was higher. He was going to come!

What a crazy feeling! He was aware of the dick in his ass, and the cock in his hand, and how balls feel in your hand, and how the guy he was sucking had pushed into a deep throat [that was just before the point he would be induced to vomit], how he was wiggling a little, how Stan was gasping and obviously was about to come, how the dick in his mouth jerked and how the warm cum felt as it dribbled out one side of his mouth ....

Thought and feeling were a combined mass of colors and sensation. Everyone stopped for a few seconds. He was exhausted and feeling better than he ever felt before. The guy he was sucking withdrew and stood, making soft groaning sounds. Kitt stood and moved away. He sat on Stan for a minute, then stood. Stan made a "Ghee!" sound.

Someone had come up behind him, and was pushing him toward a massage table. He was bent over the table and was being ass fucked. The fellow on the next table was the one who was being throat fucked in the video. He was being throat fucked again, by another guy.

*I don't want anymore now*! he thought.

The one fucking him soon came and withdrew. Another stepped up. He said, "No more," and stood. Randy came to hold him and say, "You okay?"

"Better than okay. I just can't handle more right now."

"It's after two. Want to go? It's alright. A few already left."

"Yeah, Randy. I have a lot to think over."

"Figure if it's for you?"

"It is, but so are other things. I'm like you. I want this. A lot. I also was Leo ... some girls."

"Bi is best. Doubles your chances of a date Saturday night – like you need double!"

"Anything else you want to try?"

"Yes, but not now."

They left. Everyone there knew when they did. The party was over. The guest of honor has left the building.

Randy dropped him off at Helen's. He went to his room and slept late, for him. It was almost eight o'clock when he got up.

He felt strange, but very good. He went into the kitchen to fix eggs, cheese, and sausage in a sandwich, along with a couple cups of great coffee.

He went to the park for the first time. He wanted to see if the things he'd heard were true.

They were, and they weren't. Very few of the people from the gym went there, though most of the teenagers that hung around the gym were there.

"Well, well! Imagine seeing you here!" a voice said. He turned. It was that Felon character, standing there with a boy who couldn't have been more than twelve years old.

"Wow! You're really handsome!" the kid said.

"He works at Happy. I don't know if he likes youthful guys, but he does like some things!" He grabbed Tim's crotch, and came to staring at the sky, the whole jaw and side of his face a pool of pain.

"I don't like creepy old pedos putting their hands on me," Tim was saying to the kid, who was wide-eyed.

Tim walked away as Evergreen, with another boy, came to ask what happened.

Tim had a cup of coffee at Eileen's Café and went back to Helen's. He read a book he had from Elmsville, and was getting ready to go to work when a two cops came to tell him he was under arrest.

"I am? Cool! What for? I've never been arrested before."

"Er, assault and battery."

"Really? Who did I assault and batter? Anyone I know?"

"A Mr. Felon. In the park. This morning."

"Him? He grabbed my crotch and I pasted him one. I think the first one to make contact, physically, is the assaulter? Wouldn't that make me the assaultee?"

"Er, you broke his jaw."

"And?"

"Look, we know what he is. We can't do anything about it, because none of those kids will testify. A Mr. Evergreen said he just mentioned he saw you at Happy Days, and you struck him."

"I'm night manager at Happy. Hundreds of people a day see me there. Why would I smack anyone for saying they saw me there?"

"All I know is Evergreen said he saw you attack Felon."

"I'm going to be late for work over this?"

"I have to take you in. Maybe you can post bond and get released."

"I have to go before a judge to post bond, right?"

"Yes."

"And my accuser has to appear at the same time?"

"Yes, technically."

"No technicality. Is that the law?"

"Yes."

"Then let's go for it! Maybe I can get both Felon and Evergreen off the streets for awhile!"

The cop grinned. "I won't cuff you or any of that. I'd like to see those kind of cruds in the chair, but I didn't say that!"

Tim laughed. He called Randy and said he was in jail, so might get to work late.

"Seriously?"

"More or less. It seems I assaulted someone named Felon."

"Homicide – I hope? I'll get you off. I know some heavy politicians."

"No. Just assault and battery. I broke his jaw."

"Shit!"

The cop, who was listening, laughed. "Is it true that a bunch of homos hang around that place?"

"Apparently. It seems some Homos and pedos do. After all, weren't Felon and Evergreasy there?"

The cop laughed. "You've got a point."

"Yeah, some of the guys are gay. They're *not* pedos, though."

They went to the station. The cop, Sgt. Moore, arranged for the judge to come downstairs from his office. He signed a subpoena for Felon and Evergreen to appear immediately.

Twenty minutes later Evergreen came storming in. Felon was in the hospital, and couldn't come.

"Well, this is a little irregular. You've signed a statement that certain things happened, and we need some corroboration," Judge Hanrady said. "Are there any other witnesses?"

"Er, no. I don't think so."

"Well, there were the two kids you were with. I'll recognize them, so we can ask them if it's true," Tim suggested.

"Er."

"Well, the park's just a few hundred feet away, so, if Judge Hanrady will grant, you can go with me to find them," Moore said.

"Er, well, that is, I may have, uh, you see. Perhaps we will just drop charges unless it happens again, and, uh," Evergreen stammered.

"You broke a man's jaw, and he will drop charges, just like that?" Hanrady asked. "Okay! What the hell is going on here?"

"According to the defendant, Mr. Felon, and I quote, 'Grabbed my cock, so I cold-cocked him," Moore declared. "That would put Mr. Felon in the defendant's position, if true, and would make a charge of false arrest and perjury pertinent, I think?"

"Also. Evergreasy, here, wasn't there until later," Tim said.

"Hmm. So! Bring in the witnesses. We'll get to the bottom of this," Hanrady said.

"Please! It is just a little misunderstanding!" Evergreen cried. "I drop charges!"

"You can't. Mr Felon made the charges, so he would have to drop them," Hanrady pointed out. "Officer Moore, you will immediately take the defendant to Central Park to try to locate missing witnesses."

"Be back in ten or fifteen!" Moore declared, and waved for Tim to come. As soon as they were in the hall, Moore broke out into loud laughter. "You got that pedo into a state he'll have a heart attack any minute! He's sweating like a pig. You can actually have him charged with perjury for the statement he signed, and he's gone for max. Hanrady wants him off the streets as bad as I do. He's damned rich, and we've never gotten anything that would hold up. If he gets a lawyer here before your witnesses, he'll get off."

"We can probably find the kids if they're still there."

They went to the park and to the restrooms. Both kids were standing outside. They saw Tim coming, and started to bolt. Moore said they weren't in any trouble. The judge wanted them to say if what was charged was true. Five minutes."

They went back to the court. When they walked in, Evergreen started crying.

The judge took the names and promised it would be sealed, as they were minors [one 11, the other 12].

"Ask them what you want. I'll listen. That way, if there's no charge, they can go. If there's a charge, we'll handle it with affidavit."

"You saw me swat Felon?" Tim asked the one with Felon.

"Uh, yeah."

"Why did I swat him?"

"He, uh, he grabbed your dick. You smacked him and said to keep your hands to yourself or something."

"Thank you." He turned to the other kid. "You came there with Mr. Evergreen, and saw me swat him?"

"No. We came when he was laying there on the ground and you were already walking away. You said he should keep his hands to himself or something."

"You didn't directly see me swat him? You were with

Mr. Evergreen?"

"Yeah. We were around down by the gate and Evy said we would meet Ricky there, so we went, and you were going away."

"Thanks. That's all we have to get straight."

"You can go," Hanrady said.

"Can we get the money first?" the one with Evergreen asked.

"Money? What money?" Hanrady asked.

"They said they would pay us if we let them fuck us. They fucked us. They owe us five dollars apiece. We were going to get the money when we saw him walking away."

Evergreen squealed like a skewered pig.

"Moore! Take this piece of refuse into custody. Charges by this court of sex trafficking minors. Children!

"You! Charges are dropped on all counts! You will be called to testify.

"Moore! Get contact information and they can go – except Mr., as the defendant called him, Evergreasy, who is to go into full processing immediately. Bail will be set at five million dollars. You are then to go to Mercy Hospital, or wherever, and arrest Mr. Felon on like information.

"Court is recessed."

He stormed out. Moore hauled Evergreen to his feet and cuffed him.

"Buy you a soda or something?" Tim asked the kids. They went out.

Tim bought them sodas and chips, then went to work.

He told Randy what happened. Randy said he would never fail to surprise him.

Other than that, it was a fairly ho-hum day.

Tim didn't have too much excitement for awhile, until the trial of Felon and Evergreen landed them both in twenty to life sentences. He then was known as someone who got pedophiles convicted, no matter how rich they were.

Randy came to him after the trial. "Tim, I don't know what to say. You're in a bad position here."

"What do you mean?"

"Well, the gay orgies, the gay patrons...."

"You've made it plain that they aren't welcome here if they're into even chicken! What the fuck is going on?"

"I'm getting pressure from some of them. They say you're advertising that this is a gay hangout."

"For crying out loud! I found out about it on a bus a hundred fifty miles from here! Everybody in the state knows it!

"What's really going on?"

"I didn't tell you this: Senator Phillips wants you out."

"Why?"

"He used to come here. A lot. Before he ran for senate. He thinks he can get by if no one connects, but he's on a committee that oversights those issues."

"I see. I thought you said you'd have anyone who tries blackmail hit."

"Blackmail?"

"You are to get rid of me or ... what?"

"Tim...."

"I ... can get ... Okay. I'm to offer my resignation, not be fired?"

"Tim...."

"I tender resignation as of the first of next month. That's six days."

"Tim..."

"I'll clean out my locker in five days. I want to talk with my friends about it. I want to know why any of them would 'pressure' you."

"Tim.... They didn't. In fact, a couple are outraged because anyone would suggest it.

"Tim, he can put me out of business!"

"Blackmail. I'll handle that part. I want to know ... I think the only way to handle a blackmailer is to black-mail him even better.

"Randy, I'll keep you out of it. I'll keep all the guys here now out of it."

"Tim, be careful. He's powerful with the mob. They put him there, and he owes them big time!"

"You don't know anything. Keep it that way."

Randy nodded. "Is there any way to keep the place's name out of it?"

"If I can halt it before it goes too far, yes."

Tim went to the office and ran the day's schedule to printer for the counter, checked out the multi-lift for a sticking joint [only need oil], checked the juice machines, and talked with Will and Gina, who hadn't heard any word about his testifying, except that he was applauded for getting those two rich child molesters off the street.

"Tim, we know about those two twelve year old kids.

They told their story from behind a screen and are guaranteed anonymity. We also know you don't think it's all that bad for ... the pedophile thing.

"What gives?" Gina asked.

"Pedophile? I'm hell on wheels about it. I think I just proved that in spades. I just don't consider a young teenager a child. Most of the guys here had experiences when they were fourteen or fifteen. Almost everybody does.

"If they're forced? Blow the bastard's head off! If they're curious and agree, or if they initiate it? So what?

"Those kids aren't teenagers yet, and are prostitutes. I want to know who, how, and why. I consider that the same as murder. No statutes of limitations."

"You're weird!" Will said, grinning. "You go to parties here, and we know what goes on. Then you're a big pedophile hater?"

"That's a pretty typical question from people who don't know that most pedophiles are hetero. There are a lot more homos against it, percentage wise, than heteros. Paedophilia is *not* homosexuality.

"There isn't much I haven't done on the homo end. There are a couple of things I intend to try. There are a couple of things I *won't* try. Kids, even teenagers, are no part of it."

Gina said she agreed with it, but she thought teenager, up until seventeen or eighteen, should not be exempted.

"Get real! Most kids have 'messed around' with their buddies by the time they're fourteen. That's why I said unless they initiate it."

"Can't argue," Will said. "You made me see it was

personal. I don't like even the idea, you do. Move on."

They chatted few minutes, then the classes started, and they would be busy the rest of the day.

Tim put Tommy on the counter and went back into the office and locked the door. He went to the file cabinets and checked the active member lists from six years ago until one year ago.

What he was beginning to suspect was there.

He then went into the surveillance section and took out the videos from those years.

He had what he needed!

*Senator, Sir! Ah say heah, Ah mean, Ah say it – you are goin' down! And not that way!*

He copied nine bits from the second stick and four from the third, then put everything back in the safe in the safe.

*Thirteen is NOT your lucky number!*

Two of the videos had Felon, Evergreen, and Phillips standing right beside a pickup microphone. While there was a lot of background noise, what they said was fairly clear.

Four years ago. Those kids were seven and eight years old. Would they be victims of those three?

It seemed likely.

No one else must be involved in this. If it backfired, he was to be the only one hurt. That was written in stone.

The rest of the shift was rather blah, though several told him they envied his courage in facing those two child rapists in court.

In the morning, Tim carefully wrote what was on the videos and membership records. About eleven thirty he went to the park and talked with the kids. He asked them some pointed questions. He promised everything would be like in the court. Sealed and private and no one would ever know it was them.

He soon got their answers. He recorded it without their knowing.

He went back to Helen's to transcribe the pertinent parts, then went to the gym, where two fancy lawyers were waiting.

"We're here to interview you about the court case you were involved in," Metcalf said sternly. "There are some questions of entrapment, here!"

"Fuck you."

"That is not a productive attitude!" Collins almost snarled.

"Fuck you, too."

"You will answer our questions here, or in front of a judge!" Metcalf threatened.

"I choose door two. Fuck you – and get off the property or I will throw you off."

They were suddenly uncertain. They exchanged looks, and Collins said, "We just want to clear up a few points, then we will go."

"You will go *now*!"

"Look. We got off on the wrong foot here," Metcalf whined. "We pulled the act and it didn't get a booking in Peoria.

"We really do need to get some questions answered."

"Then ask them. I promise to answer anything you ask, even if it's just to say, 'Fuck you! It's none of your goddamned business!' No subterfuge – and I'm recording it all, as you definitely will be."

Collins let a small grin flash across his face.

"I'll ask first, then Dan can cover anything I leave out," Collins said. "I know you aren't going to answer the first: Who are the supposed kids that testified from behind the screen?"

"As you suggested, I won't answer that. I'll just say they weren't even close to the only ones who can confirm the charges. They were the only ones we needed. They aren't 'supposed' kids. They *are* kids."

"Why were you in the park? Were you cruising?"

"I was crossing the park. Like the chicken, you know. To get to the other side.

"I don't cruise the park – or bus station, or airport. I pick up tricks at the gym, which is known for that, the same way a lot of them are, or people I meet in any number of places, like restaurants and stores."

"You are admitting that you're homosexual?!"

"I'm bi. I pick up women as well as men.

"*Men.* I'm not into boys. As demonstrated, I'm very definitely against messing with children. The women are *women*, not young girls."

"Er. Men like Mr. Felon? Mr. Evergreen?"

"*Men.* Not child molesting flabby out of shape fops."

"Um. Well, we just wondered if you were there to meet a ... well, that Mr. Felon mistakenly felt you were after, er, that is, um!

"Dan? Anything?"

"No. He's onto us.

**Page 58**

"Tim – may I call you Tim? – we're here because it's our job. Some of us don't like the methods we have to employ." He pulled a recorder from his pocket and turned it off. Collins looked surprised, and did the same. Tim put a book over his mini-recorder, right there on the counter. Collins giggled.

"We hate this, but it's what being a lawyer entails, anymore.

"Do you have anything else you're going to spring on the shits we're working for? Someone is running scared out of his mind, because you work here. He thinks you might be able to show something he doesn't want known."

"Like the times when he was a member, and how often he spent time here?"

"Well! That answers *that*!"

"Doesn't the idiot asshole realize he would just have to not say or do anything, and it would be forgotten? Is he really that stu ... Ah! He gets Felon and Evergreasy off on some silly technicality, or word gets out?"

"Something like that."

"Does he know Randy's policy about blackmail?"

"Policy? Blackmail?"

"Anyone who tries to use anything from here in blackmail gets hit."

Metcalf roared! He was laughing so hard he was crying.

He pointed to his recorder and turned it on. Tim moved the book.

"Well, Tim! You *do* surprise me no end! You are a very practical person!"

"I'm pragmatic, if what my friends say is true."

"We wasted the afternoon with this, but that's fine with us! We get paid, results or no!

"I wish you a great and pleasant day. Hope you find the perfect man – or woman – to make it end pleasantly!

"Come on, Colly. We got shown how the system works."

They waved and left.

Tim wasn't fooled for a second. He knew exactly what they were there for, and he knew he got his message delivered.

He won that round!

Nothing much happened for a week, then a car almost hit Tim as he walked to work. He saw the car parked down the block when he came out of Helen's, so he kept it in the corner of his eye. At 3:30 in the afternoon there was usually nobody on the street, certainly not in a car where there was a yellow curb.

The car suddenly spun out as he stepped off the curb to cross the street. He stepped back, and it almost hit the curb. It kept going.

When he got to work, there was a call for him, so he answered, to hear, "You have been warned!" and the phone cut off.

He went back to the office and made a call to a number from the old records. The phone was answered by a secretary. Tim said, "Phil. Tim calling."

"Mr. Phillips is in conference, and cannot be disturbed. Would you care to leave a message?"

"June twenty seven, twenty fifteen: That one will cause us trouble. You should be careful. Nine years old, and right out there in public? That woman didn't believe for a second you were checking to see his fly was zipped! You're a fool!

"Rather distinctive voice, huh? Full video available at this address, along with place and participants."

He rang off.

Nineteen minutes later, he got a call from a different phone with caller ID blocked. "I got your call. What was it about? You didn't make any sense!"

"As I said, 'Rather distinctive voice, huh?'

"Now *you* have been warned. The full video is in a safe place, with copies in other safe places. Do anything that stupid again, and you're gone.

"In fact, do anything to get your two asshole buddies released, and certain things will become public knowledge.

"You're a fool! The cameras in that room are right there, and obvious, and you stand right beside a sound receptor?"

"But ... but ... the cameras are turned off when we ... I mean you can't ... Oh, shit!"

"Thank you for confirming the video." He rang off.

The phone rang again. "What's the deal?"

"No deals. If that dog's woken up, it's *you* who didn't let it lie."

This time, Phillips rang off.

*Between a rock and a hard place, for real! Them or me. See who's got the most to lose!*

Tim went through the schedule and posted two new members, then went out front to find Collins standing there.

"You hired the hit car?" Tim asked.

"No. Is that what happened? My client called in a panic and said I was to make a deal. Any deal that would give him some room."

"Yeah. I called him and told him that was a stupid thing to do, seeing I had the records of when he was here when Felon and Evergreasy were. I also let him know there were other records of those times, and even a complaint that he was trying to pick up a young boy.

"This place has a fixed, inalterable rule about that."

Tim had actually found that in the files.

"I see. The reason he wants those two excrescences out is because he's the same pile of shit.

"Well! I argued with you until you actually moved to throw me out in the street, physically! No deals! Not now, and not ever!"

"Something like that. Maybe I should act like I actually will. There are two people who have been hanging around for the past two days that are not members, and who I've never seen in town before. The woman was, shall we say, seen loitering near my place of abode."

"You're big enough I'd get the hell away from you if you threatened me in any manner. Try to not mess up my suit. I hate the thing, but it's a lawyer uniform." He laughed.

Tim put out his arm toward Collins and moved toward him. He turned around and cried, "You *assaulted* me!"

"I didn't touch you. *Yet! Get out!*"

He headed for the door at "An accelerated pace" and was gone. Tim went back into the office and had a good laugh. Collins had managed to look terrified. Very convincingly!

*Well, Phillips, I think I won that round, too!*

Tommy came in just before closing time. Randy left early on a date. Tommy asked Tim to sleep with him.

Why not?

The bedside radio alarm woke them up, and the radio news was on.

"...when Senator Phillips said it was all a lie, and that he was resigning to insure that other innocent people weren't drawn into such a sordid situation.

"Senator Ardmore, with the ethics committee, said the material that was delivered to him surreptitiously was damning, but that it had to be authenticated. There is much in the news lately of false charges, backed by altered video and audio recordings.

"In other state news, The Champions for Peace rally was interrupted when..." Tommy turned it off.

"You?"

"No. I wonder how ... maybe it's not from here. Maybe it's about something else.

"I wanted to make life total hell for him, like he did to some of my ... others, then destroy him."

*What does Tommy know? How did he know I had anything?*

*Now I'M the one who's confused!*

He asked Tommy.

"A few of the guys said they didn't like what was happening to you. You're one of the greatest personalities, plus the best bed partner, we know. We aren't going to allow it!

"Randy told us about him being threatened if anything got out, and that he was to fire you or his father and mother might have accidents.

"Tim, he can't have anyone know he had anything to do with our getting that video of him with Felon and

Evergreen. They'll kill his parents, and him too! That's why he went to Elmsville. To protect them. Carl and Kitt and Gene went with him. That's why he wasn't there to close last night."

Tim got out of bed, put on his clothes, and was heading out the door. Tommy asked what he was going to do.

"What I should have done the minute I found that video."

"Tim?"

"You're not part of it. Randy isn't part of it through his own fault. None of the guys are part of it.

"Tommy, I love you. I love all the guys.

"Stay out of it! If they threatened Randy's parents, they'll threaten mine. That's going a lightyear too far!

"I hope to be able to stop him before he gets out of the state. There's no place on this Earth he can get away from me!"

He stormed out, went to the lockers at the bus station to get some material there, and turned around to find a man standing there.

"I'll take that!" He showed a pistol under the newspaper on his arm.

"There are four other copies."

"So?"

Tim shrugged and held the memory stick out. When the thug reached for it, the lights went out for him. Tim was fast and accurate. Tim sat him on the bench and walked out as he slumped over and sprawled on the floor, the pistol just out from his left hand. As he reached the door, he heard a woman scream.

He went directly to the police station, where Moore was just coming on duty. He said to get Hanrady there as fast as possible.

Hanrady was in his office, so they went there, where Tim tossed the 8 GIG memory stick on the desk, and said it was self-explanatory, due to the recent events in Hanrady's court.

Hanrady gave Moore a questioning look, and Moore shrugged.

The memory stick went into a USB port on the desktop. Hanrady clicked on the video icon.

It was Felon, Evergreen, and Phillips at the club. Not much beside the date and time, and a few rather simple things in the background, like a 69 on a massage table and a guy getting ass fucked on a sofa. The sound was no good.

"We suspected he was gay. We couldn't prove it. We didn't dare act," Moore said. "Just gay, who cares?"

Not much could be heard, except when Evergreen said, "Fourteen ... too old ... not ... fuck."

"Hmmm," Hanrady said. "Iffy. We would have to have more than that to act.

"This why the SOB resigned this morning?"

"A little part of why. I want to stop him from running," Tim replied.

Hanrady clicked on the second, where the three were standing next to the sound receptor.

"... to do something that stupid. The kid was only eight years old, but who would have thought he'd tell his mother about getting fucked! She's going to bleed me! I just know it! She doesn't give a fuck about him. She's a lush," Felon was saying. "God! How could I not see it?"

"You're stupid. I'll agree to that!" Phillips replied. "I'll have them haul her to my office, and tell her we're investigating you people, and that only part of it was true.

"She'll be drunk. She always is. I'll tell her we'll have to hold her in protective custody, if what she says is true. She'll know she can't get booze, so will say she was probably exaggerating things.

"What about that little Ames boy? He's what? Ten? And already hung like a horse! I think he may be experienced."

"He likes it. He charges five bucks," Evergreen said. "I've trained him. It's been almost a year, so you know he's not blabbing."

They discussed a little girl, eleven years old, who was into it. Phillips said he wasn't that much into girls, but what the hell.

Hanrady was red-faced, and furious. "Get my aide in here! Warrant form. Statewide. Immediate!"

He clicked on another file. It was the one with four incidents on it that were recorded with fair sound. It was about the nine year old boy they held down and all three fucked until he liked it. Hanrady threw his inkstand across the room. He called the TV station and said to get a reporter over there, fast! Senator Phillips would be going down – hard! Anybody else they found who was trafficking in children for sex had better get out of the states and to someplace there was no extradition agreement!

The woman he was talking to yelled for Anne and Vince to get to Hanrady's office ten minutes ago. A voice called for just bare audibility that Senator Phillips was on his way to the airport, where he had a private jet. What was he running from?

Hanrady hung up and punched a speed dial number. It was on speaker: "Federal Bureau of Investigation. May I help ... oh! Hanrady? What's the skinny."

"Do not let Phillips get on that plane! You'll have the warrant in two minutes!"

"Handy? Phillips? Plane?"

"He's running. I've got it all. He's trying to get out of state. He's heading for the airport."

"Hold on. Evette, is Sam still on SS with Phillips? ... Have him detain Phillips before he gets aboard the plane to ... I'll deliver the warrant ... on information ... the court. A police investigation ... I don't know.

"Handy? Charges?"

"Child sex trafficking. Multiple counts. Two others, minimum. Long term. As young as seven years old."

"Are you *serious*?! *Phillips*?!?!"

"As serious as fourth stage cancer."

"Done! I would have maybe believed a sixteen or seventeen year old, but seven?"

"Probably even younger. We have proof of that young. We have kids under twelve who are male prostitutes, right here in the park.

"Ah! Here's the warrant! I'll sign and fax. One minute!"

"We'll tag the bastard. You want him in your court?

You did get the evidence. Ongoing probe?"

"I've been after those [even too bad for me to print] for years. I finally got them! – or a police officer and citizen did."

There was nothing to do now, but wait. Tim and Moore went to Dinah's for coffee and heated Danish.


Phillips and a man called "Evans" and one called "Peterson" were locked up. Felon and Evergreen were included, and had many added charges/convictions. None of them would ever get out of prison.

Prison time didn't go easily for child sex predators. They would learn how it felt to be raped and tortured. Repeatedly, with no end in sight.

Happy had a surge in business when it was learned that they were behind the breaking up of a pedophile/child sex trafficking ring. The newspapers and TV made it a point to show that pedophile and homosexual were two different things, and that homosexuals were *less* likely to be pedophiles.

"We'll leave that stuff to priests and preachers," Kitt was quoted.

Tim went along much as usual. He met several people he really got along with, and a few he didn't. Leona wanted his baby. He was undecided, because he wanted to be a father like his, and that wouldn't be possible.

Or would it? He could be the same, open, honest, non-judgmental type person. He could be as pragmatic as his father.

He told his father he was laying with more men than

women, that he would probably not be a father.

"You really should be. You've got good genes. From me? Probably not so good, but your Mom has the best in the world!

"If you're not, you're not. Your brother and sister carry the same genes. They're both married.

"You sucked a dick yet?"

"Yeah. A few. I really like it. Before you ask, yeah. I've been ass fucked. It's okay, but not really my thing. In an orgy, you do all kinds of things you thought you never would."

"Sort of jealous. Never been in an orgy."

They had no secrets. He didn't go into details, but he didn't lie if asked. Pops didn't ask.


He had a little fling with a girl he'd laid when he was sixteen. Her husband had died in an automobile, well, truck accident.

He went back to Evanston after a vacation weekend back home. He slept with Tommy and Randy the first night back.


Three years. Tim had been to two of the orgies, and had slept with a lot of guys. He had a long talk with Leona about having a kid. She admitted she didn't much care for sex, and it didn't bother her if he slept with a hundred guys. She would probably be hurt if he slept with another woman. [They got married to make it legal, and she had, over three years, a son and daughter. She was a great mother, and Tim was with the kids a lot. He got to be lot like his father.]

There was to be an orgy tonight. He thought about it, and decided to go. He had done almost everything, and there wasn't much more he wanted to know. He had a full [well, a lot more than that!] sex life with what he knew. There was nothing ... yes there was!

"I'll be there! It might be fun."

He went in with Tommy and Carl. Things were already into the second stage when they arrived, and they went right into it. He watched as some got off. He had those videos [and would have more tonight] of that, and was really turned on. He had seen lots of videos of *him* getting off. He knew what they expressed wasn't phony.

He had a few romps. He sucked two guys he never had before, and was sucked by them and others. It was mostly the foreplay bit, and he was getting as hot as the first time. He wanted this to be a first time.

Who?

Ben Sharp had a really nice cock, the size he could handle, just a hair before too much. Vince and Kent were doing the tongue all over bit, and he was getting to the colors and sensation stage in bursts.

Ben was sucking Harry on the massage table to the right. Tim laid on the next table, where Ben was closest to him, and laid his head partly off the end, while someone was slowly sucking him and someone was licking his nipples.

Ben turned around, and he reached back and put his hands on Ben's hips to draw him to him. He took Ben's prick in his mouth and started sucking slowly. It was to

Ben to supply the motion, and he pulled him ever deeper into his throat.

He came here tonight to get throat fucked, and it was happening! It was crazy, because he couldn't control it. Ben was getting into it, and was moving deeper and deeper, until it was as far as possible. He pushed harder and held, without moving, for a few seconds, then was fucking slowly. Tim had to push him out after a couple of minutes, to where he could breathe. Then it was back. Ben was going a bit faster, and was making the sounds of deep sensation.

He was coming. Oh, god! This was wild! Ben was coming! It was colors and background noise that was almost music!

Ben pulled partway out. Tim was sucking very lightly, and was also fondling his balls. Some one else was sucking him. Now Ben was moving slowly deeper again.

He wasn't designed for this! His whole body was about to explode!

Ben came again, and was backing out. He'd had all his body wanted, for the moment.

Tim pushed the one who was sucking him away, and went to the bar for a tequila and grapefruit. The bartender said that was some show. He didn't even know he was jerking off until he came!

"You don't know a tenth of it. I've never done that before."

"But you'll do it a lot more now! You *really* got off!"

"Probably not. I'd be disappointed. It was the best I ever knew, and it can't happen again.

"To tell the truth, I think this will be my once in a lifetime experience to remember forever."

Tim and Leona wished Nicole well, and watched her get in the waiting taxi. She had a full scholarship to a major university. Randy, their son, was already attending a major university on a full scholarship.

"Your Pops always said we have great genes," Leona said. "I guess, like in everything else he said, it's true.

"I wonder why neither of our kids are gay, or even show any interest in it. I'm frigid, and you're bi.

"Ain't life weird?"

"Well, *we* are! Pops also said some are and some aren't. That's very damned well true!"

"Want gumbo for supper? I don't think you've met him yet."

"Always willing to try something – or somebody – new!"

They went back into the house, laughing and joking.

For the rest of his life, he didn't change very much, except for the mellowing out and inability to "perform" at the level he did when younger. He was healthy to the end, as was Leona. They died just two months apart. Him first, then she willed herself to die. She – and he – accomplished a lot in life, and they were in love much deeper than they ever knew. She didn't want to live without him. She knew, deep down, that his great love for his "buds" was real, and fulfilling, and that it didn't take anything away from her. She was naturally non-sexual.

Well, she did miss him in bed with her, after awhile,

even though sex wasn't part of it.

They were both in their late seventies. They had a lot of very good productive years together. The rough spots weren't, really. Charmed lives.

He had a lot of romps with guys, thousands, if you figured it, but he never had another throat fuck.

One does not try to outdo perfection.

C. D. Moulton's works are available on most major outlets as printed or e-books. CD writes the CD Grimes, PI, mysteries, the Det. Lt. Nick Storie mysteries, the Clint Faraday mysteries, the Flight of the Maita science fiction series, books on orchid culture and many others of many types. Mystery, adventure, intrigue, science fiction, humor, fantasy, paranormal, mild erotica, and factual.